Evincepub
Publishing

Evincepub Publishing

Parijat Extension, Bilaspur, Chhattisgarh 495001
First Published by Evincepub Publishing 2020
Copyright © Dr. Satyanarayan Mishra 2020
All Rights Reserved.
ISBN: 978-93-89988-41-3

STATUE AND STONE

Winning Wings And Other Poems

Dr. Satyanarayan Mishra

About The Book

———•••———

This is the fifth English poetry book of the poet. The book contains poems of various types. The poems have their typical poetic composition each carrying some short of message. All the poems bear the feelings, sentiment and themes touching the heart of wide spectrum of readers. Structured with simple words and sentences the language is not at all difficult or clumsy to grasp the contents. Evincepub Publishing has done a great job in giving these poems to the form of a book. Hope that readers will appreciate the job.

About The Author

———•••———

Dr.Satyanarayan Mishra is born in Puri District of Odisha. He has published lot of poems and stories in various journals and newspapers.

His other published books are:

Staring at the sky, Come down please, A wild flower and other poems and Epitaph of the falling tree.

Contents

Dr.Satyanarayan Mishra

Am I Cheated

Give me some donation
yells the beggar
what donation? nothing, nothing, go away
Mother, please give me an old cover
It is shuddering winter
I have no old cover
Said the lady
I tossed it out,
what is the utilization of keeping old and detached things
Alas, It would have been helpful for me,
Murmured the poor person.
Wait, I will offer it in the coming year -the old cover
It is new now, so cannot donate
Said the mistress.
At least give me a few rupees,
I may not get your cover next year

Why? asked the dignified lady.
Mother, am too sick, may not live long
Told the poor.
So, what amount would I give you?
Asked the lady.
If it is not too much of trouble, give a hundred rupees.
It is unreasonably less than I need still, told the poor
person.
Oh, take it and leave,

We will meet and talk one-year after
The mistress assured.
The beggar quitted joyfully,
Am I cheated...? asked the lady herself.

———— ❖ ————

Dr.Satyanarayan Mishra

Do You Want To Hear

Do you want to listen to the song of the cuckoo
the hum of the bee or the harsh sounds of crow?
What do you want to hear?
the music of nature or that of stream flow?
Does not it sound well the dripping sounds of rain?
Do you not like to listen to the crying sounds
of agony and pain?
Do you not want to hear the giggles and laughter?
It may please you, dear, the sound of a wild creature
Have you listened to the whispers of love?
Have you ever tried to hear the mourning dove?
Have you noticed carefully the sound of lapse of time?
The tick-tock of a watch and the victims of crime.
Do you ever try to listen to the pulsation of the heart?
the nerve impulse of the body, how to do you like that?
The planets smile, stars twinkle, tells something new.

Statue And Stone

The flower and plants of your garden
 also the morning dew
Nature has the sounds of her own may it appear odd
However, listen carefully to the inside story
 it may be the 'Tale of God.'

———•———

Dr.Satyanarayan Mishra

Experience

Six men went to see an elephant
Every one of them was visually impaired
Initial one contacted the broadside
What is more? he told it is only a Wall
Second, caught the tusk
Described, an elephant resembles a lance.
The third contacted the squirming trunk and
suggested, it is a snake as it were.
Fourth contacted the knee
To him, the elephant was only a tree
The fifth one got the ear
Alas, the creature is a fan like.
The last one got the tail

Statue And Stone

Oh! Brother, it is a rope as it was.
So, like the perception experience varies
Description also turns fancy stories.

———◆———

Exploring New

When I thought of exploring new territory
Be that as it may, I discovered touch all over the place.
Wound down to reveal to something new
Could not locate any untold story
Endeavored to sing a perfect work of art
Alas, it was ever heard
Profoundly wished to portray an image
Nothing so, everything in nature drawn
Asked me….
Am I mixed up?
Puzzled by the misery of everything achieved
Then, how new manifestations develop every day.
Every day with another hope, a blossom with a new
aroma
A ballad with new message and emotion,
a picture with so engaging

Statue And Stone

Furthermore, you too, appearing
new, adorable consistently like
the recently married bride, a new gleaming moon and
another desire for me to give inspiration all along.

———◆———

Dr.Satyanarayan Mishra

Inside The Temple

The kid went to a temple
Appealed to God for some cash
The priest inquired
What did you implore?
The kid replied -money.
The second day he went
Supplicated devotedly, Requested a home
The priest asked...what this time?
A home...the kid, said...
I got some cash yesterday
The third day he went
Prostrated before the symbol
If you do not mind, give me a lady
Hey, what did you implore this time?
I acquired a home yesterday; presently I need to wed.

You will no uncertainty get that.
In any case, my dues...asked the priest
What dues Punditji.I played a joke with you
I did not get those, hope to get,
Then why do you come here every day?
The kid showed towards a young lady who occupied in revering.
Means? ...Asked the pundit.
I come here not for divine beings but rather to see her.

———◆———

Dr.Satyanarayan Mishra

Naughty Illustrations

———————• • •———————

When I attempted to depict an image of a stream;
it resembled a surprising green line
Tried that of a sea
Only a blue fix.
Decided to draw the plants and woods
It appeared like some rich green illustrations.
Again attempted to shading the skyline
with a downpour bow
Only could draw a band of seven groups of shading
not all that exuberant
Attempted and tried to bring sky, stars, and world
I could not, all were either hued patches
of brilliant specks or shade
Attempted to outline the morning sun
Red light as though was there
Fish, fire, tiger, lion, so wonderfully I tried

Statue And Stone

Be that as it may, those were murky, lifeless illustrations.
Asked my partner, why such occurs with me?
Where goes the enthusiasm
which was regularly stunning
in my tyke time illustrations
She told...your eyes have changed,
so adding the discernment.
Lost guiltlessness—
so what might you be able
to draw more.
Finally, I endeavored to draw the image
of my exquisite accomplice
Gracious… see, how it looks...she exclaimed...
It is precisely a moon
no less quick than a stream
and no less stunning like a streak of lighting...
I smiled...She said
You are extremely naughty.

———◆———

Dr.Satyanarayan Mishra

Oh!My Toys

Past playing instruments of my youngster hood days
I remember, how to dress you, feed you and kiss you
Organized you in various styles
Oh!My toys
You are not with me now
I have become old and
You are lost in oblivion
I have never stored your remaining parts in chronicles
I can precisely not recollect on which day I got separated
from you

Statue And Stone

Maybe a developing sign in my body or psyche could
intrude on our connection
you are as yet alive in my memory and heart
Oh! My toys-My earlier days playing accomplices
Maybe you were my best instructors
I figured out how to sustain my toy like children
I figured out how to be a toy and manikin in the family
and encompassing
You instructed me that silence, that speechless kinship
Despite everything I cherish you my toys
When I enter a toy shop now
I look through your resemblances.
However, the shop owner says, those are obsolete.

———— ◆ ————

Past Paints

Oh past, give me a relief
believe me, I am not your fan
nor the lover of your topic
I enjoy your enchanting encounters
When I get time
But most of the time the pains remind me
How was the I, the worst victim!
Many awards, rewards, pleasure, and glee
you have no doubt shared with me
But at times of your ghast attack
I fumbled with the bent knee.
Oh Past, I love you even,
No matter you were cruel or kind
But I fear you when unknowingly
You try to push into my mind.

Statue And Stone

Past is past, will never return
It was a part of the time I spent
It was somehow full of tragedy
Somehow with little paint.
Be kind to me Oh, Those days
Teach me the lessons of life
Give me the strength to face
Days as sharp as knives.

———◆———

Dr.Satyanarayan Mishra

Statue And Stone

He was so great, so popular
We remember even after death
We made a statue of him
In which exist his soul and breath.
We made a stone for him
To see him alive always
We garland him every year
Remembering his working days.
We regard him, worship him
As if he is a god-like
He was a great man

Statue And Stone

We speak loudly in mike.
We find the stones everywhere
Falling around his statue
All these were living memories
Stones sing their virtues.
Pains and struggle make one strong
as robust as stone.
Curse and torture make one die
Breaking his muscle and bone.
A Statue and Stone ....no voice then
only they stand and gaze
Had they been able to return and come,
no one may further praise.

Dr.Satyanarayan Mishra

What If

What if the things would not have happened
If the world would not have been created
Nor the creatures, plants, animals
What if the sea and the stars, the sky
and the lands would not have existed
What if, there would not have been
any evolution, any civilization
Imagine no sun, no moon, and galaxy
would have been there.
then what if we, you and he or she
would not have existed
...no nothing would have happened,

Statue And Stone

Let all collapse, nothing will happen
only conservation
We exist, that we believe that is life
Let us enjoy now
with what we have
not with what if...?

Dr.Satyanarayan Mishra

When Eyes Begin Talking

When eyes begin talking
Something starts
The quiet talk and a major begin
Heart begins pulsating
Dreams show up and vanish
Lips look at each other
The ear hears something new
A tone drifts in the vacuum reverberated with the
sentiments
A spring begins shading the nature
A mumble grooms
A bloom grins welcoming a margarine fly
A progression of incidents, then and after
Oh dear, the eyes investigate
each other energetically
Inquiries the individual inside

Statue And Stone

A joy blasts out.
Tears of grasping spirits
What a feeling, an ecstasy
An interminable involvement in mortal world
Alas, the eyes should dependably stay this way
As though prepared to begin talking.

Dr.Satyanarayan Mishra

Zoo Diary

Inside the walled-in area
He took a gander at the fence
wall of the zoo
Where he stayed for long.
He was dozing, sleeping, yawning
No activity here, where he is a show
A show for visitors, who come and visit the zoo
He recuperated while he was an offspring
In the thick woods, somehow his mom had abandoned
him, and the foresters had rescued him
He was a kid lion
Be that as it may, he had overlooked the specialty of
jumping, running, attacking
In the next enclosure
another lion arrived a couple of days back
Oh dear, you will endure like me as well.

Statue And Stone

Here is food; here is cares yet no family, no opportunity
Occasionally he meets with the lioness
As the zoo experts like.
Be that as it may, the lioness and cubs are in other
enclosures, or sold to different zoos.
The new lion in next fenced in the area looks at him
tries to compromise perhaps
No business...idiot,
you are in prison, being as well.
A guest tossed some biscuits, nuts and fruits
into the enclosure,
He murmured...I don't take all these, except non-veg,
May I kick the bucket in starvation.
Somebody hopped into his cage, with a camera,
perhaps will take a selfie
The lion jumped, caught at his neck mildly,
the individual shouted, he did not slaughter
only a gentle bite, just somewhat signal of assault.
Hello, I am a lion, do not meddle in my business.
Now, the guest lion in the next enclosure
took a gander at him.
How seniors behave here, he must learn.

———•———

Dr.Satyanarayan Mishra

Mend Or Change The Trend

Oh, I endure a lot......
It's neither damnation
nor a decent place to dwell
You may not like, I think
it's no way better than hell
Here money counts always
Humanity lags,
I landed in flesh and bone
this place is not so kind
O Man.Why grumble? dont think
That society will favor
Never accuse your luck or Nature
will always add flavor
Even if everything is right too,
there may be a hostile neighbor,

Statue And Stone

It's your kin, not a wild creature of woods
keeps you scared ever.
You are the king of your wishes,
but it is not a fact
You are fascinated by your
Alluring desires, who care for that?
Nothing will happen,
If you leave your most favorite body even.
Mend or change the trend
Then only it can be thought of as heaven.

———◆———

Dr.Satyanarayan Mishra

It's You

Have you ever seen intensely yourself?
In mirror or still water
It's your image so beautifully reflected
So soft as if made of butter.
Have you ever shout in forlorn park
Or river side or jungle corridor
The reverberation sings your glory
Your story, As a mark of honor
See the pleasure, bliss,In a beggar
When he gets a coin from your pocket
It is no way lees worthy, less valuable
Than a Costly locket
you are not a discarded entity
of useless life and birth
Rather a bright star of sky
Who will glorify the mother earth.

Nothing Unusual

It's usual to get upset no doubt,
events go in their way
Nothing unusual about,
what can be to avoid the sway?
Smiling lips usually keep mum
if there is nothing to smile,
Beating bands stop their drum
if there is no festivity of style.
Lightning ceases, wind halts
if no vapors or drops,
So also life enjoys the reprieve
it's full of win and flops.
Usually usual, as usual, it is

Nothing to capture it long,
Memory plays trick, puzzles the mind,
playing the melancholic song.
Hear only the different tunes,
not be overturned by it.
Smell, taste, dance and enjoy,
inclined with it least.

Leave Me Please

I found a place where I breathe easy,
Please leave me alone, am bit choosy
I chose a good life, good air, and water,
Chose nice humans with whom I shall feel better.
I run after money, but not beyond my needs.
I seek honor too not for none of my deeds
I love family, society, animals, stream, and zoo.
I need good companion not a tight life too.
See now the collapse of bonding viral death trap
Unlucky to find me in a time, where everybody needs clap.
Everyone is possessed in work, who cares for whom?
Where remain the feeling and support,

where did I groom?
Am I an unwanted guest, not worthy of this life?
Is this planet, full of robbers having hidden knife?
Excuse me then, still, I love myself and my birth,
Bless me or grace me alone to fight for this good earth.
Give me please to make the life better for me and other.
Leave me please to break the taboos, let me march
further.

———◆———

Winning Wings

The 'End' is definite
As designed by destiny
as like as birth
But none can hinder to overrule the divine design
and draw the curtain earlier.
A lamp burns with oil, quivering flames
in the gusty flow of wind,
Resisting the callous collapse
a desire to burn and light
as if the lighting is a duty.
Fortune may be foe, circumstances hostile,
Everywhere, everything even not
Adding fuel curiously
for your life or enlightenment
rather degenerating,
depleting your existence every moment

But what are they, who are those,
are they deciding your days or know
whether one day you may be ruined and broken.
Better they should know,
none is a champ nor a looser,
one day you may come with flying colors.
Stop perceiving obliteration capriciously
Before the splendid golden sunny rays
touch your winning wings.

————•————

Please Give Me A Kiss

Do you love me, really,
am not only in your body, not only in your mind
I am overspread everywhere;
I pose sometimes rude, otherwise kind.
Sometimes I give you nectar, overflowing from
dimensions surrounding your existence
I love you too, I don't, know
how you accept my nuisance.
Those poisons you isolate in my whole span
it's worth of your only deed.
Unfortunately, you condemn me, alas;
I can't calm for you my speed
You treat me as enjoyable senses
depleting your elixir of life.

Dr.Satyanarayan Mishra

How can I check your hands
when you touch your neck with a knife.
Unknown always
why one compares with other beings
Did the scriptures tell or teach
such silly, harmful things.
I am a bubble; I am a cloud,
life of overwhelming bliss
This time ,I am with you,
Oh man, please give me a kiss.

———◆———

Oh! Idiot See Me

He was roaming by the side of the track
absent-minded he,
Couldn't know what he was searching,
Something unknown to me
With tearful eyes, scared he was
He, a home left guy.
Or was searching for job,
food, money, like a child for a toy..
He was waiting for something, I did not guess,
what his job on track is.
Was he to leave for someplace
or a mind blank.
Suddenly the whistling train
as soon as ran fast.
The fellow boy was looking anxious
he was breathing fast.

Dr.Satyanarayan Mishra

Suddenly a mad man jumped on the track
pushed the boy by force..
Oh idiot see me, am still alive
why choose such a course?
The boy got the sense, recovered after,
people gathered around him..
Searching there the mad was absent,
running far from the team.

———◆———

One Plant One Life

Do not think, do not assume, it is granted forever
Don't throw into the garbage before tasting the flavor
Things which comes easy to one's hand always loses cost
it may never come again, never happen
after it turns to dust
It's a spark like lightening for a moment be
Realize the value, realize the essence it's not an offer free
one plant, one life, one flower or a stream

Who gives the right, who gives you the freedom to destroy
the life's cream?
it may be a dream, may bea flash, maybe a twinkle of a
star
Never throw it into the debris, value is nothing at par
It's not counted in achievement, not even in success
It's your attitude; it is your acceptance indifferently to win
and losses.

———————◆———————

Neither Nor

Neither it rains nor does the Sun radiate.
A standstill atmosphere prevails
Neither the sky is clear nor is it overclouded
Everywhere the race somehow trails
Neither the winds blow fast nor it is inert
the moon too neither rises
Never the life recovers to a lively pace
With too much peace and prizes.

Dr.Satyanarayan Mishra

Weather

Sometimes it confuses
neither good nor bad.
Then it can't be called a cool
refreshing or mad.
Often the wind flows unevenly
turning its mood to stormy,
The moon ruptures the sky frame
downing the psycho gloomy.
The stars appear covered
as if by some dark curtain,
No way has the weather looked appealing
or with a gesture certain.
The ocean gets baffled
the naughty waves collide,
They try to cross the shore
with armors of the tide.

Statue And Stone

The oceanic voyage seems tough
when someone looks at the sky
the wind of storm, rain and cloud
create a fear to cry.
At this juncture of life
the soul needs some support.
Don't know your friendship of which weather
Only you can report.

Dr.Satyanarayan Mishra

Speechless

One day I saw you in Park
What a beauty queen endowed with a spark.
I could not tell what I was feeling,
Your presence made others too thrilling.
You were as bright as a star,
I felt no way at par.
You were looking like the moon,
I could not recover my sense soon.
I pretended as if knew nothing
when you looked at me,
I was shivering, speechless with glee.
Alas, I always go to the park, never find you again.
I propose for you presence nothing more than that then.

Evening Here

Evening here approaches
with a cloudy sky, foggy weather
In fact every evening has some specialty...
Some new unique touch, let us feel it together,
For a moment forgetting the uneven reality...
Every evening the stars promise a lot,
the moon peeps or not, guessing her orbital location
Every night comes with a dream in a knot,
reveals or not depends on mood & situation,
Every night promises to give a handful of enchantment,
but maybe it turned to a nightmare,
Every promise makes a race in mind,
making the heart pulsating with hopes be bad or fare.
Every moment I pass even
can't always be a promising,

Dr.Satyanarayan Mishra

Still to digest even the hardest time
Sometimes I avail the evening
My beloved waits with patience
Eyes full of tears,
I don't know these tear drops
are either of pain or pleasures.

———•———

Why Do You

Why do you love
it's beyond my perception.
Either any motive is there
or some foul deception
Sometimes you look curiously
at my body contours, I don't know why
What's there it's as usual anatomy
even an animal has what is there for eye?
Often you appear naughty
I don't understand what for
I am not a toy or beast in zoo,
why others bother?
The discrete difference between love and lust

I can't discriminate sure
if at all its a disease I think
what may be its cure..
Do love and lust coexist ever
in reply, I say 'no'
love is divine, lust is bodily
one high, one low.
If you love me unconditionally
I say,I too do same,
if you pretend the desire
do not try to tame.

———— ◆ ————

Whatever Be The Outcomes

My mind is a wandering bird
difficult to locate its wings,
Difficult too to predict its movement
also the mood swings.
It's a pretty cat sometimes
waiting eagerly for a fish,
Even if no hunger
still, it expects invitation for a dish.
It sometimes coalesces with wind
flows dynamic with the storm,
Never have I been able to perceive
its structure or its functional norm.
At times it speaks with a low voice
trying to convince me with logic.

I don't know where it drags me
with what enchantment of magic.
It where sleeps in my body
where it awakes to action.
Sometimes it persuades too
to involve with some fiction.
As long as I try to pet it
wilder it becomes.
No need to calm it always
may whatever be the outcomes.

———◆———